CHESS FOR
BEGINNERS:

A Complete Guide to Chess Fundamentals and How to Play Chess Like a Pro and Win Every Single Match

Antonov Myers

Table of Contents

Introduction

One thing one should know is that chess is a game of skill, and like any skill, it can be learned. If you are earnest in learning the game of chess and improving, it will take some efforts on your part to take time and study the game, analyze your sets and play A LOT of games to improve. One of the most popular games for ages has been chess. While some people may know how the game of chess is played, there are some rules for beginners that can make the learning process a little bit easier. While the game might appear overwhelming at first, you don't need to worry; it is straightforward to learn, but will take a lifetime to master. We will look over some of the basic rules about chess pieces and other elements of this timeless game.

To begin with, we should look at the fundamental elements of the game. The chess pieces are broken down into a two-color scheme. Usually, a traditional board will use black and white figures. In a few cases, you might find that the colors change, but there will always be a light and a dark option. The individual who plays with the lighter color goes first. The board is made from 8 rows that have eight squares running along with it. Depending on the board you own, they will alter between black and white. Each player will have two rows on the board that contain the chess pieces in their possession. There will be eight pawns for the front row, two rooks that look like castles, two knights that resemble horses, two bishops, a single queen, and an only king. On your side of the chessboard, you will place the eight pawn pieces in front, with the back row containing the rooks on the edges, with the knights next to those, followed by the bishops, and in the center of the back row the queen on the left and the king on the right.

With this in mind, we should quickly look at what each of the pieces can do for you and how they move. First, pawns are not only the necessary chess pieces you will deal with, but are one of the most important ones for you to understand as you learn the chess rules for beginners. These pieces can move one or two spaces on their initial move and then a single square forward on their consequent movements. They can only go ahead until there is no other piece in front of them. To capture another player's chess pieces, your pawn needs to be diagonal to that piece.

Rooks can move any number of spaces forward, to the back and on either side. They cannot jump pieces and can only capture items in a direct line.

Knights can move in an L shape only. You can take them 2 spaces forwards or backwards and then one square to the left or right. Think of the letter "L" when you do this. For some, this can become one of the trickier chess rules to remember. This is the only piece that can hop over other pieces.

Bishops can move diagonally and can only capture items in their direct line.

The queen is the most powerful of all pieces, and she can move in any direction and capture a piece in any direction, but it cannot jump pieces, unlike the knight.

The king is your piece to protect. You have to keep him safe. He can move a single space in any direction. You cannot move him into the danger zone. He goes into check, if placed in the capture direction of any piece of the opponent. If the king has no safe move to make, he goes into checkmate situation, which ends the game and you lose.

The main aim of the game is to capture your opponent's king while protecting your own king. This is quickly done by capturing the chess pieces of your opponents.

With these vital elements in mind, you can begin the game of chess; but remember that beyond the chess rules for beginners there will be other elements you will need to learn. Nothing can replace the experience playing more games against different opponents. Once you play your first game, the second one, then your third game, you will begin to find what playing style you are comfortable with and start dominating your opponents.

Chess is a two-player board game; one player plays with white pieces, and the other one plays with dark pieces. Every player starts with 16 pieces and takes turns moving one piece at a time across the board.

The opponent with the light pieces goes first. You can think of your chess pieces as your army of soldiers who are going to battle. The primary aim of the game is to attack your opponent, eat as many of their parts as possible and eventually trap their king, in a position, that is called checkmate.

While your main objective is to trap your opponent king, this may not be the case for every game. There are other ways in which a game can end: one lane is a dead-end where no opponent can control the other OR when a player king is NOT in check but is stuck in such a way that no matter where he goes, he can check for himself, which is not a legal decision.

Another form of deadlock is when the two opponents have captured all the pieces of the other EXCEPT for their kings. It's a dead-end because you can't just subdue the kings on the board.

The last and final way a game will end is if one player throws a towel and quits. Although you should never leave the game, you can do this by merely knocking over your King and letting your opponent know you're going to stop.

The reason you're never supposed to leave the game is that you never know what's going to happen, and all it takes is ONE mistake from your opponent for you to take over the competition.

One quick tip: the one who controls the center four squares controls the game and is in a stronger position to attack. So, keep this in mind when you're playing your first game.

If the chess beginner attempts to apply a specific aperture to a real chess game, they usually get unstuck as their opponent makes a non-book pass. It's best to learn ethical opening principles first, which will help you to change your openings based on your opponent's moves.

1. <u>Control the Center:</u> The first idea is to control as much of the middle as possible of the chessboard. The central squares are d4, d5, e4, e5. It will occur naturally for whites for most openings, the two most common opening moves being the queen's pawn moving to d4 or the king's pawn moving to e4.

2. <u>Build your Pieces:</u> Moving your queen's or king's pawn first, gives you a chance to control either d5 or e5 and also makes space for movement of the other essential pieces. Put in the second theory of creating space for your main pieces, beginning with your Knights, followed by the Bishops. You may need to move another pawn to build your Bishops ultimately.

    Moving your Knights to either C3 or F3 will help protect your advanced pawn and control more of the middle of the board.

3. Castle Early:

   You can have Castle as soon as possible, preferably on the Kings' side. This helps defend your King from an attack and releases the Rook to the Center of the area.

4. Connect your Rooks:

   Once you have Castled, you should move the Queen to allow your Rooks to link and move freely in the back row. But push your Queen with care, as another first concept is not to over-expose your Queen.

5. Create a Solid Structure:

   Don't be tempted to attack until your pieces have been created. Your aim in opening the chess is to create a stable foundation from which you can attack your opponent.

By upholding these rules, the chess pieces will have more freedom of movement and will be less vulnerable to attack.

If you're familiar with these ideas, you can learn a chess opening or two, and if your opponent doesn't follow the book moves, you can fall back on these concepts as the next thing to do.

Most beginners have placed too much focus on mastering chess openings, just to be disappointed when their opponent doesn't obey the text. Others will spend time exploring the Endgame only to find that they never get there. Too frequently, the Middle Game in chess is ignored, but it's one that can help make up for lack of experience in the openings and give you the advantage of the Endgame.

Chapter 1: How to Set up the Board

Configure a chessboard correctly without breaking the sweat

Chess is a fun and challenging game. But before you can play chess, you should know how to set the board for the right match.

Chessboard level

The main thing you have to do is make sure your page is set up correctly. With a blank board in front of you, there should be a white space in the bottom right corner, no matter which side you are on (in white or black pieces). At first glance, this may seem like a choice, but the position of the chessboard is one of the most essential parts to make sure the chess boards are in the exact place.

Put the pieces

Now, when your screen is in good condition, you can add your tracks. In this example, we'll assume you play the white pieces, and your opponent has the black parts. We will also consider regardless of whether you can differentiate between one piece and another, or if the chess players have a standard design. Keeping this in mind, looking at the bottom row (the row closest to you on the board), the pieces should be placed in the following order from left to right: rook, knight, bishop, queen, king, bishop, knight, rook.

Rooks are parts that look like a castle or a cup. The knights look like horses. Bishops are pieces with a "frown" groove on top. The king is the most noteworthy piece and has a cross above it. The queen is the second tallest piece with a "crown" above it.

By your rival (dark sides right now), the setting is nearly the equivalent. The main distinction is that when you work from left to directly with dark pieces, first comes the king, at that point, the sovereign.

You will learn to check this in just one second quickly. Of course, for both sides, the second row at the bottom is full of pedestrians/pawns - they are the shortest piece on the board.

As mentioned earlier, chess is a classic strategy and technique match. It is a war game that is played on a 64 square board with alternative colors. These squares are called bright and dark squares. The pieces are usually black and white, and the white moves first at the classic beginning. Each side has 16 pieces, as follows:

Eight infantries (soldiers)

Two rooks (castle)

Two bishops (priests)

Two knights (guard)

A king and a queen (Royalty)

To alter the chessboard, set it up so part of the board moves before you with eight squares to one side and right.

Configure your pieces as follows:

In the bottom row (close to you):

Put a Rook at each end.

Going down the middle, place a bishop next to each rook.

Now place one knight near each bishop.

Spot the king on the square to one side.

Put your queen in the last square.

In the row in front of the Rooks, Bishops, Knights, 8 pawns are placed one on each square, from left to right. The task of the infantry is to protect the king at any cost.

One approach to recollect where the king and queen will be placed is to put the lord on the OPPOSITE field of shading. If the king is white, he will be in a dark field. If it is black, go to the light field. It's the same in every case.

Special rules

You may not move your king to "check."

If the king is "controlled," it must be compensated or prevented from being arrested without regard to costs. If the domain has no movement to protect it or remove it from the danger of being captured, "Checkmate" is announced, and the game is over.

Double your work before you start the game

Since the time pieces are on the board, the exact thing you have to do is a twofold check to ensure they are all in the opportune spot. Since the king and queen are the most significant pieces (and a few sections are frequently not unfilled), you need to ensure where they are.

A fast and simple approach to do this is to take a gander at the circumstance the sovereign is in. He should rest in a square that has a similar shading as him. Inline, the lord goes to another square. Toward the end, when everything is set accurately, the ruler and the contrary sovereign must face each other on the chessboard.

Match the chessboard with the chess pieces

One of the best things about chess set is that there are no rules. All things considered; this is something you can do to find a set of chess pieces on the chessboard instead of looking for the chess set you've already collected.

There are still a set of guidelines that can be followed to make this process quick and easy for you.

Match the size of the king to the board

The first thing to consider is the diameter of the king's base. The king is the ultimate chess piece and therefore has the largest base diameter. The primary purpose is to make that the chessboard is larger than the base diameter of the chess pieces. It's good to leave it.

For those who want to improve, the standard rule is that a square chessboard is 33% larger than the king's base diameter. So, if your king is 1.5 inches in diameter, you should have a chess target with a 2.0-inch square (1.5 inches' x 1.33 = 2.0). Of course, you can choose 1.75 inches, and it looks great, but you probably don't want to go too far.

Match the color of the pieces with the chessboard

The second thing you want to know is how chess is formed. Particular attention should be paid to chess pieces and metal.

Chess pieces provide the most fundamental rules. Chess pieces made of rosewood work best with chess boards with dark rose and rose. Black and ebony chess boards match chess boards like color. Shamsham (a light brown wood) is best with paintings of walnut, hazelnut, and shisham. Wooden tiles are the best matte or matte satin tiles, but they can also be glossy.

Metal chess pieces match three different chess boards. Chess and metal pieces are very similar to plates pressed with rice, both traditional rice and a type of color such as blue and red. Also, these pieces go well with wood boards that have a glossy finish, especially gray wood planks. Finally, the metal chess boards are well defined by the compressed leather chess panels.

Commanding the Puzzling Knight

The knight has a specific pattern of movement. They are described as an "L-shaped" model. Simply put, the knight combines rook's and bishop's moves. The rook moves in a straight line, and the bishop goes diagonally. The knight establishes a short distance between the two, and does more than any of them.

The knight has certain advantages in moving in his model. There are only nine moves you can make from the center. The knight can jump over other pieces. He is the main piece on the chessboard that doesn't have an immediate vision way and the way he experiences.

The knight can reach other besieged chess pieces and remove them even before they make their first move. This makes the knight as a black OPS in your chess game. The rest of the chess pieces cannot follow him. It is a warning to be careful about how you use this piece. Make sure you are extra careful when using it. He may be the only one who saves the game.

The knights can't hit opponents far, but they can fall on them slowly and cunningly. Like the pawn and the king, the knight is limited in his ability to move and attack. You understand that you must learn to use this to your advantage so that the game moves to the checkmating of the king.

Sometimes it never changes. The knight can change the play in record number of moves by landing on the opponent's field. It is how to attack all sides and is no different from the knight. He can attack and capture the same number of pieces as any other piece.

Knight is a black OPS in your performance (chess strategy). It is a game you need to think about carefully, using the wisdom and experience of chess to become the most crucial competitor and chess player.

Using puzzles to develop chess brains

Puzzle chess helps train the brain to find opportunities for its army to attack the enemy, as well as identify the same type of threat from the opposite side against the army.

Tactical Puzzle teaches you how to identify short-term opportunities to attack and capture enemy material. Of course, you should be aware of certain types of chess tactics, such as pine, fork, pumpkin, and discovered attacks.

Checkmate puzzles give you another type of test - these help you find opportunities to capture the enemy king character, which is the ultimate goal of any chess game you play.

If you haven't tried a chess puzzle before, these might seem like a little secret ... "What are we going to do with them on the field?" ... "How does it work?" And so on...

Before we get stuck, there are things we need to know if we have a chance to solve many of the chess puzzles ...

Know the pieces and expertise the moves

While you are not trying to play a complete game, you must still be able to identify the infantry and five different pieces (knights, bishops, rooks, pawns, and kings). Also, keep in mind that not all of these units will be present simultaneously in the puzzles you are trying to solve.

In addition to recognizing pedestrians and parties, we have to know their movement patterns, as this helps us analyze specific situations - in the puzzle and determine who is the candidate (s) who needs to move.

Comprehend the notes of logarithmic chess

In chess, movements and other actions are recorded using the system 'Algebraic Chess Notation'. If you are not sure about this, a brief review should help you along the way.

The chessboard is divided into 64 squares, and each square is given a unique code or reference - if you are surprised, the program works in a similar way to the network reference system you receive on the printed maps.

Here's how the squares are named or numbered on a chessboard:

| a8 | b8 | c8 | d8 | e8 | f8 | g8 | h8 |

| a7 | b7 | c7 | d7 | e7 | f7 | g7 | h7 |

| a6 | b6 | c6 | d6 | e6 | f6 | g6 | h6 |

| a5 | b5 | c5 | d5 | e5 | f5 | g5 | h5 |

| a4 | b4 | c4 | d4 | e4 | f4 | g4 | h4 |

| a3 | b3 | c3 | d3 | e3 | f3 | g3 | h3 |

| a2 | b2 | c2 | d2 | e2 | f2 | g2 | h2 |

| a1 | b1 | c1 | d1 | e1 | f1 | g1 | h1 |

Next, we have to learn the unique identifiers for pedestrians and parts, as they help us to record which square the piece moved to:

N = knight

B = bishop

R = rook

Q = queen

K = king

Based on what we have learned so far, if we are to say that a bishop was transferred to the field "f5", we record this movement as "Bf5".

However, pawns do not receive a large letter. The only way to tell if a pedestrian has moved is not to have a large letter. All that is recorded is the square reference, where the pioneer completed his move. For example, "b4" means that the pedestrian has been shifted to "b4".

What you just saw is how we use it to solve chess puzzles ...

To solve the puzzles, we must express the movement in the same way we record movements with algebraic notation. If you think the queen's solution is heading for "h3", you can say "Qh3" in response.

However, this is not just a movement. It may be paramount to specify that our solution includes other types of maneuvers, including capture and infantry.

Chess puzzles are not only a logical way to pass the time, but are also tools that can be used to sharpen the chess brain, which helps cope with the potential threats that maybe faced in the game of chess.

Chapter 2: How the Pieces Move

The Chessboard

The most basic thing that you are required to learn in chess is how to set the board up. The rule here is always **'White Is Right,'** and that means, when you sit in front of the board, the bottom right square should always be white. If you are playing on a board that folds in half, you must always play across the fold as well. The set up for both the black and the white pieces is the same:

- The rooks or castles must go on the two corner squares on the bottom row.

25

- The knights, or horses, go on the squares directly adjacent to the rooks.

- Next are the bishops, and they stand beside the knights.

Your queen must always go on the square that matches her color. You will have two squares remaining at this point, so the white queen goes on the white square and the black queen on the black.

The remaining square on the bottom row is for the king.

This is your first row, or rank, on the chessboard. The pawns are placed on the next row of squares in front of the bigger pieces.

Chess is played by two people using a chessboard with 64 squares of alternating colors, eight rows, and 8 columns. Each player starts with sixteen chess pieces: 8 Pawns, 2 Knights, 2 Bishops, 2 Rooks, 1 Queen, and 1 King.

Here is how the chess pieces are arranged at the start:

The rows are called 'ranks,' while the columns are called 'files.'

Pieces and Moves

The two sides are called White and Black. Each side has sixteen playing pieces, of which eight are 'Pawns' and the remaining eight are called 'pieces' (Pawns normally aren't). Black sets up the same way, except that the order of king and queen are reversed; each player starts with his queen on his own color; White Queen on a white square, Black Queen on a black square. The pawns are placed onto a square all across row 2.

General Movement Rules

Each side moves one and only one piece or pawn per turn. (There is one exception to this, called 'Castling,' which will be discussed below.) A move must be made at each turn. At the start of the game, the White player makes the first move. (This gives White a very slight advantage.)

In the formal play, touching a piece or pawn obligates the player to move that piece or pawn (but not to make any specific move with it). Also, in the formal play often there is a time limit on chess moves; a player must move before the timer runs out or forfeit. In informal games, this is seldom observed, and a player may take as long to move as desired.

Moving a piece or pawn into the same square as one occupied by another piece or pawn of the same color is not allowed; only one piece or pawn may occupy any one square. Moving into the same square occupied by another piece or pawn of the opposite color, removes that piece or pawn from the board, and replaces it with the moving piece. This is called 'capturing' or 'taking' the enemy piece.

Knights can move through (or jump over) pieces and pawns of either color to reach an allowed open square. All other pieces and pawns cannot move through squares that are occupied. A capture ends the move; a capturing piece must end by occupying the square previously held by the captured piece.

Capturing the opponent's king ends the game, but in actual play, the king is never captured. A move by a player that puts the opponent's king in danger of being captured on the next move is called 'checking' the king or placing the king 'in check.' This must be announced. Normally, the player making the move simply says, 'Check,' to notify the opponent that his king is threatened. A move that places or leaves a player's king in check, so that it will be captured on the opponent's next move, is not permitted. That is, if there is a way to move the king out of danger, the player must make that move, and if a move would allow the king's capture, the player is not allowed to make it.

When the king is placed in a situation where it is threatened with capture on the next move, (in check) and there is no move open to the king's player that will prevent the capture, this is called 'checkmate,' and means the game is over.

Pawns

The movement of pawns is governed by a few rules:

Pawns move into open spaces only, forward along with the file they start in.

Pawns cannot capture with a forward move. Instead, pawns capture diagonally and forward. That is, if an opponent piece occupies the squares to a pawn's left or right in the rank one square ahead of it, the pawn may capture it. If it occupies the square immediately ahead of the pawn, the pawn cannot capture it and the piece blocks the pawn from moving.

Pawns can move only forward, not backward.

On its first move, a pawn can move two spaces forward or one. Thereafter, it can move only one space forward (or forward/diagonally when capturing).

If on its first move, a pawn moves two spaces forward and lands on a square that to its right or left there's an opponent's pawn, the opponent's pawn can capture the other pawn by moving diagonally to the square that the other pawn just passed.

If a pawn moves to the eighth rank, that is, to the opponent's side of the board, it can be replaced by any other piece. This is sometimes called 'Queening' the Pawn because a queen is the most popular and common piece to turn a pawn into when that is accomplished.

Bishops

Bishops may move only along diagonals. This means that each bishop always remains on the squares of one color, white or black (each player begins with a bishop on a square of each color). Bishops may move any number of squares along the diagonal, subject to block and capture rules.

Knights

Knights exercise a complicated move that can best be described as an L-shaped jump. The knight 'hops' either one or two spaces forwards or back, along with its file, and then one or two spaces left or right along with the rank so that it moves three spaces total.

As already noted, a knight may 'jump over' any pieces, friendly or enemy, between it and its final destination, provided the square where it ends its turn, is either empty or occupied by an enemy piece, which is then captured.

Rooks

The rook moves forward or backward, left or right, along the files and ranks. It may not move diagonally. It may move any number of squares in any non-diagonal direction, subject to block and capture rules.

The Queen

The queen is often called the most powerful piece in the game. It's like a rook and a pair of bishops combined. It can move forward and back, left and right, without limit, just like a rook, and also can move diagonally like a bishop (except that the combination means it's not combined just to one color). Its movement is subject to block and capture rules.

The King

The king, like the queen, can move forward and back, left and right, and diagonally, subject to block and capture rules. However, it can move only one square per turn.

There is one exception to this, which is called 'Castling.' Castling is also the only time that a player can move two pieces in one turn. The two pieces are the king and one of the rooks. In order to Castle:

31

Neither the king, nor the rook can have already been moved during the game.

The two or three spaces between the king and the rook must be empty.

The king cannot be in check, and the Castling move cannot move the king through a square where it would be in check. (And of course, the move cannot end with the king in check, either.)

The player wishing to Castle, moves his king two spaces towards his rook, and then moves the rook adjacent to the king on the side opposite of where it started. Thus, if the White player wishes to Castle using the rook that was closest to the king, he moves his king from e1 to g1 and then moves his rook from h1 to f1. What Castling does is to place the king into a more protected position where it is (often) guarded by a row of pawns and cannot easily be placed in check.

Chapter 3: Strategies for Opening the Game

Opening Moves in Chess

Theoretically, you can start the chess game with any move, as far as it is a legal move according to the rules regarding the movements of the pieces. The first move, which is known as the opening move, should be a good move as it gives you an edge over the opponent, as you have an upper hand with the good opening move. A better opening move allows you to protect the king, to make utmost use of the vital squares, to move the pieces in the desired direction, to swap and capture the pieces as per the rules.

After studying the game of chess for many decades, moves are provided with a name, to identify the moves without much difficulty. As I will be explaining the famous opening moves that have been repeatedly used over the years, I would recommend laying the chessboard and placing the pieces as it will be easy to make the moves and understand the situation as is being explained.

Preparation is the key if you want to win in a game of chess. This is why you must start the game by taking the right steps. This is where opening moves come into play.

How Are Opening Moves Advantageous?

Although playing chess does not require a person to know an opening move to play, one obvious advantage of knowing about opening moves and employing them is that it enables them to place their pieces in a position where it could contribute to the development of your game plan. Opening moves also sets the player's defense against the opponent's game plan. By starting the game with calculated moves (and not just making random moves), it will be easier for them to apply different tactics, control the board, and improve their chances of winning the game.

Types of Openings

Openings can be divided into four types, depending on the pieces involved in your first few moves. These opening types are the following:

34

King or Queen Pawn Openings

Being the pieces at the front of each side during the start of the game, the pawns are usually moved first. However, the most common would be moving the pawns directly in front of the queen and/or the king. For White, their d and e pawns will be moving to the fourth row. Aside from providing an open space so that bishops can be deployed early on, the king or queen opening enables the player to gain control of the center area.

Gambit Opening

A 'gambit' in chess refers to a strategy wherein the player is offering 'bait' (which is often an undefended pawn) to the opponent. This bait aims to entice the opponent into moving differently to gain a lead in developing the player's pieces. A gambit opening can be of a queen's or king's, depending on which side the bait originated. For example, if the opponent (who's playing Black) matched your pawn to e4 move with a pawn to e5, you can move your King's side pawn to f4, allowing Black to capture the pawn. If Black accepts the gambit, it will bring a development advantage to your side because you can now do a 'Queen Pawn Opening' to square d4 and further control the center. A gambit opening can also be used in combination with the other openings mentioned in this section.

Flank Openings

If, suppose you're playing White and your opening move doesn't involve moving the king and queen pawns first, you are doing a flank opening. Pieces that are included in flank openings include moving any pawn on the queen and king side (squares a to c, and f to h, respectively) or moving either of the two knights.

Irregular openings

Opening moves that are rare and are not always observed in a game can be considered as an irregular opening. Mostly irregular openings involve the movement of the pawn that does not take advantage of the 'two square moves' from their starting position.

By knowing the first moves of your opponent, you will have an idea as to the game plan that they are trying to accomplish in order to win the game.

White's Opening Moves

White has the advantage of making the first move and being able to set the pace of the game. Thus, the right preparation must be made if they want to improve their chance of winning the game.

This section will discuss some of the basic opening systems that can be employed by White.

Colle System

This opening strategy, which can also be called the 'Colle-Koltanowski' system, was formulated by Edgar Colle during the 1920s and was improved by George Koltanowski.

The Colle system stemmed from the Queen Pawn Opening, and features the following moves (ignoring the moves of the opponent):

- Move queen's pawn to d4

- Kingside knight moves to f3

- King's pawn to e3

- Bishop on f1 moves to d3

- Kingside castle

- Castled rook moves to e1

- C pawn moves to c3

- Queenside knight moves to d2

- Pawn in e3 moves to e4

This image will help you to visualize what the board should look like when using the Colle system (before the pawn in e3 is moved to e4):

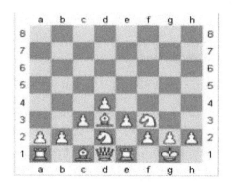

The order of the movements can be interchanged, as long as all pieces are in place, within 9 moves. The Colle system allows for a good way to develop your minor pieces (the knight and the bishop), gain some control of the center with the d4 pawn and a threat from the f3 horse on any piece that will occupy e5, open paths for your non-pawn pieces (especially the queen), and move the king away from the center as early as possible.

Reti System

Another opening system that was developed earlier than the Colle system, but is still an effective opening method is the Reti system. Developed during the late 1800s by the chess player Richard Reti, this opening only involves two moves for White.

- White moves g1 knight to f3 (Black will most likely move its queenside pawn to d5).

- White's c pawn moves to square c4.

In the Reti system, the board must look like this:

In this opening system, it is easy to observe that Reti applies the flank opening and combines it with a gambit, making use of the 'wings' rather than a direct approach to control the center area. The movement of White's knight to f3 forces Black to avoid making the usual e5 pawn opening. If Black moves its queenside pawn, the c4 pawn will be offered as a sacrifice to the opponent. Even with the early lead of Black in material (if it chooses to accept the bait), White will be provided with different opportunities. Since Black's center control is gone due to the shift in direction of its pawn, White can take control of the opponent's half of the center board by simply advancing its pawns to d4 and e4 and no Black piece, to immediately stop those moves. Another advantage would be that White can opt for an early check and a fork on the undefended pawn, forcing Black to make a move that does nothing to develop its other pieces.

Many other variations or defensive movements have stemmed from the Reti system, making it difficult for opponents to predict what you'll be doing in your succeeding moves.

London system

This opening system was named as such because it was mostly used during the 1922 tournament in London. This system makes use of the queen's pawn opening but does not combine it with the queen's gambit (which is a common opening move). The system shares similarities with the Reti system in the sense that it also develops the knight early on, followed by the queenside bishop.

The variations of this system depend on the moves of Black. However, if Black's movements are ignored, this opening system can be applied by doing the following moves:

- Advance queen's pawn to d4

- Knight in g1 moves to f3

- Queenside bishop moves to f4

This image shows what the board looks like if the system was successfully used:

The use of the London system presents early advantages on the side of White. First would be the obvious advantage of using the queen's pawn opening, which leads to automatic protection to one of your pawns. Another is that the second and third move easily develops your kingside knight and queenside bishop, allowing you to check on other pieces that Black would want to develop, making the opening system also usable by those who are looking to attack. The pawns on c2 and e2 can also be advanced one square as the game progresses, allowing you to bolster your defense in the center and protect the king (aside from castling) while giving you room to develop your remaining minor pieces and the queen.

Stonewall Attack

To prevent your opponent from getting to your king, you will need to provide a good defense. If you are interested in a defense-based game plan, what you need is the Stonewall attack opening.

This system also utilizes the Queen's Pawn opening, but doesn't utilize the Queen's Gambit. But along with the queen's pawn, this system involves moving the other pawns in the center in such a way that they are protected, either by other pawns or the minor pieces. The pawn's position in the center also allows for open lanes so that White can also guard any attacks from the flank.

To execute this opening, the following moves must be followed:

- Queen's pawn to d4

- King's pawn to e3

- Kingside bishop to d3

- C pawn to c3

- F pawn to f4

If the moves are followed properly, the board must look like this:

Using the Stonewall attack allows White to guard whatever it is that will come to the center square with its pawns, allowing it to capture opponent pieces that will attempt to occupy the said area and provide the pieces with enough protection. This makes it difficult for Black to penetrate White with a direct approach. Unfortunately, flank attacks are also checked by the White's long-range pieces. And even if Black does manage to start an attack on the king's side, it can easily be shut close by the pawns in columns g and h.

Let us look at other Openings described by algebraic notation.

English Openin

'Flank Maneuver' is the other name of the 'English Opening,' which has a unique opening such as: 1. c4

The attempt to take control of the center is made by White, through taking charge of the sides. Whereas c5 is the option left for the Black as a counter.

The King's Indian Attack

To give a sound reply to the King's Indian defense, this attack is played to gain an edge over the opponent. The sequence of play is:

- E4, d3 (white pawn moves in e4; white pawn moves in d3)

- Nd2, Ngf3 (white b-knight moves in d2; black g-knight moves in f3)

- G3, Bg2 (white pawn moves in g3; white bishop moves in g2)

- 0-0 (castling on the king's side)

The White has an upper hand with these moves. The Black will look to employ moves as "The French Defense" or "Sicilian Defense" to tackle the strong opening move of the white. Nevertheless, Black cannot surpass the White, as the opening move is stronger to tackle the counters of the Black. The center may witness a harsh play, as many pieces could be lost in the attack for both the players.

The distinct feature of this opening is that it has a capacity of being played even in the middle of the game, and not just at the beginning of the game. The Black should have a foolproof strategy to fight back against the white,

44

who can use this counter to a defensive of the Black. This counter will help the White to proceed an all-out to the king of the Black.

Alekhine's Defense

This move came into play in the year 1921 and is considered as a hypermodern move of defense which includes moves such as:

E4 Nf6

The move opens the door of being aggressive for the Black. Such a forceful move makes White form a broad pawn formation to tackle the attack of the Black. Black makes use of the opportunity to gain a lead by attacking the White pieces. The opening of the White can be neutralized by such an effective Black attack. Equal chances of winning are available for both players with this move.

Caro-Kann

The Black gives space to White to capture the center as the Black makes a move to the d5 by employing the pawn. This opening is just like "The French Defense" with an extra move. The moves to start with are:

E4 e6 (white pawn moves in e4; black pawn moves in e6)

D4 d5 (white pawn moves in d4; black pawn moves in d5)

Nc3 dxe4 (white knight moves in c3; pawn in d5 captures pawn in e4)

The pawns of the White are attacked by the Black, to bring in play his pieces to take control of the board. Such a move is not a part of "The French defense" if comparing both the openings. Black will end up playing a passive game with the hope of White making a minor mistake to get into the game again.

Center Counter

The 'Scandinavian Opening' is the other name of 'Center Counter' that opens with:

E4 d5 (white pawn moves in e4; black pawn moves in d5)

The next move will mostly be: exd5 Qxd5

Price or Modern

Commonly known by the names such as 'Price or Modern,' it is started with either of the following two moves:

E4 d6 (white pawn in e4; black pawn in d6) (OR)

E4 g6 (white pawn in e4; black pawn in g6)

The variation of the Modern Defense can proceed with:

D4 Bg7

In the 1930s, this move was considered an ineffective move. But, since the 1960s, the risk-taking players have played this move. The white is given a chance to make use of the center by the black, to outsmart the white in the process. Such a tricky move needs a lot of courage, as the center is not in the control of the player.

Roy Lopez

'Spanish Opening' is the other name of 'Roy Lopez.' The three initial moves in this opening are:

E4 e5 (white pawn moves in e4; black pawn moves in e5)

Nf3 Nc6 (white knight moves in f3; black knight moves in c6)

Bb5 (white bishop kingside moves in b5)

The name of the opening is derived from a Spanish clergyman who lived in the 16th Century, as he was a true enthusiast of the game. It is considered as one of the pioneer moves in the early days of chess. Lopez used to record the moves in his notebook after closely studying the openings of chess. He has used over 150 pages for the documentation of openings in the history of chess. Even though this move has his name, it is considered to be an older move that was developed even before he was born. The proof to the statement is that, this opening move has been mentioned in a Gottingen manuscript of 1490.

Only because of Baensch, a Russian Theoretician in mid of 1800, this move came into existence again, until then Lopez opening was infamous. Many grandmasters make use of this opening, as it is a preferred move of the present generation players.

A potential pin is enforced by the White by making use of the d-pawn or knight and the castle is activated as the open attack is launched. The Black is forced to move its e-pawn to d4 by the opening of the White.

Giuoco Piano

This type of opening move is also known as the 'Quiet game.' The Bishop of the White is used for the attack. The counterattack by the Black is done easily by making use of moves such as:

E4 e5 (white pawn moves in e4; black pawn moves in e5)

Nf3 Nc6 (white knight moves in f3; black knight moves in c6)

Bc4 Bc5 (white bishop moves in c4; black bishop moves in c5)

The game becomes passive when the White tackles by moving to d3. Such a move is known as 'Giuoco Pianissimo' or 'The Quietest Game.'

The move can be "Evans Gambit" when the White moves to b4, instead of d3. This move facilitates the exchange of pawns to get access to the center of the board and the queen's bishop is unlocked and ready for action.

French and Sicilian Openings

These are the simplest and the most basic openings.

French Opening-Defense:

E4 e6(white pawn moves in e4; black pawn moves in e6)

Sicilian Opening-Defense:

E4 c5(white pawn moves in e4; black pawn moves in c5)

Before bringing into play any of the pieces, make sure you think out the response and counter to the response of the move. The above-mentioned moves are the various openings and counters used throughout the long history of chess, and you should be well versed with them to master the game of chess.

Chapter 4: Middle Game

The middlegame. This is what separates the good from the great. Anyone can memorize opening lines and opening traps, and endgame mastery is almost purely technical and can be learnt over time. The middlegame however, is where the artistry of chess lies, and this is the chance for you show others how good of a player you really are and how well you understand chess positions.

In my opinion, how you should approach the middlegame is based on general strategies, the type of opening you play and the type of player you are.

The middlegame is where the chess battle really begins. In the middlegame you basically have 2 main options. You can either try to:

- Win material so you can win the endgame

- Attack your opponent's king and checkmate him

Of course, your opponent isn't going to let you win material or checkmate them so easily.

In fact, pretty much the first thing any player does when they are deciding what move to make is to check that their move isn't going to allow their opponent to win material or checkmate them (of course you should be doing the same). So therefore, trying to hit your opponent with an obvious plan such as "trying to capture their pieces" or "trying to checkmate their king" is unlikely to work a lot of the time, especially if they're a strong player. Instead, we can try to do other, more subtle things to gradually improve our position and make it easier for us to eventually win material or checkmate our opponent. This is called coming up with a "middlegame plan". Some examples of more subtle things we can do to improve our position are:

Gain space by advancing our pawns - This gives us more freedom for our pieces to move. More space = more options for our pieces = more opportunities to win material or checkmate our opponent.

Advance our pawns and try to promote one of them to a queen

Gain activity for our pieces - We developed our pieces to central squares in the opening but they're probably not quite in the right position yet to attack our opponent. This is where we get our pieces more active by getting them further up the board (but not too far up the board otherwise they might get trapped by enemy pieces) or try to open up lines for our pieces by exchanging more pawns and giving our pieces more freedom to move. We also want to limit the activity of our opponent's pieces of course by blocking them with our pawns (or even better, forcing their pieces back so that they are blocked by their own pawns!)

Fight for control of the centre - In the opening we fought for control of the centre briefly, but our main goal was to develop our pieces. The middlegame is where the fight for control of the centre really begins. If you eventually manage to control the centre you'll have a lot more space for your pieces and you're be able to dictate the direction of the game.

Attack with your rooks down an open file (we'll talk more about this later)

Attack your opponent's weaknesses - Usually this means attacking your opponent's weak pawns (again we'll come to this later)

Checkmate your opponent - Yes, you can still try to do this, but only if the position is right for it

All of those were examples of middlegame planning. Learning how to plan well in the middlegame is a key part of becoming a better chess player, and later on in the chapter we will show you some examples of middlegame plans and how to use them in your own games. As you practice middlegame planning more and more you'll get better at choosing the right plan to use at the right time - and you'll recognize when the time is right to switch plans.

Firstly, though I want to move onto the other area of the middlegame which we are going to practice and it's a very important one. Remember that at the beginning of the book we said that the two most important areas of chess to practice if you want to improve as quickly as possible are practicing tactics and practicing endgames. Well, right now we going to practice the first of those - tactics.

Middlegame Strategies

The middlegame is the phase when the players start to attack their opponents' defenses. Players generally form attack plans based on the game layout after the opening moves. This is the phase when most combinations are unleashed by either player to achieve desired gains. The middle phase is a test of the creativity for each player. It is a deciding phase where many games are won or lost.

Although you can't memorize variations in the Middlegame the way you would in the opening game, you will find the following principles useful in improving your play:

Exchange pieces if you find your position cramped. This simplifies play and allows you to move your pieces more freely.

Exchange pieces if you have the advantage in material but don't exchange your pawns. Pawns become more precious in the middle to the endgame.

Attack your opponent's unprotected pawns to lessen your endgame threats.

Exchange your piece if it is idle or in a bad position. Idle pieces can get in the way of tactical plays. Simplify and increase the mobility of your pieces.

Secure the center before launching offensives on the flank.

Coordinate your pieces and prepare them for tactical opportunities.

Be alert for opportunities to use combinations and tactics. Look for weakness in your opponent's development and unleash applicable tactics.

Unless necessary, avoid moving the Pawns in front of the castled King as this will compromise your defensive position.

Practicing Tactics!

Firstly, what is a tactic? There are basically two types of thinking in chess - the first is tactics and the second is strategy. Tactics are short-term calculations and strategy is long-term planning. A tactic can be a short 2-3 move combination which wins you material or checkmates your opponent (sometimes tactics can be much longer - you might be able to see a 10-move combination is you're a really strong player). Strategy on the other hand is when you think longer-term about things such as where to place your pieces, what you'd like your pawn structure to be, and what you'd like your long-term plan to be. Making a strategic move might not help in the short-term but it might help you 20 or 30 moves later in the game.

Both tactics and strategy are important - but it's more important to learn tactics, especially if you're a beginner. The problem with learning strategy is that you can spend a lot of time trying to learn strategy without really improving your chess skill. Learning tactics on the other hand will help you improve your chess skill very quickly and is one of the most time-efficient ways to improve your chess skill. In fact, practicing tactics and practicing endgames (which we'll get onto in the next chapter) give you the most bang-for-your-buck in terms of chess improvement versus time invested. Spending a lot of time learning strategy is only really worth it for top players. In fact, you could become a top chess player just by becoming really good at tactics and not knowing much strategy - but there are no top chess players in the world who are really good at strategy and really bad at tactics.

Practicing tactics will help you see and find more opportunities to win material or checkmate your opponent. Even more importantly, practicing tactics will help you see your opponent's threats and ensure you don't make a mistake and allow your opponent to win material or checkmate you. The more you practice tactics the more moves ahead you'll be able to calculate so that eventually you'll be able to see 4, 5, 6, 7 or even more moves ahead. I'm about to show you lots of different tactics which you can use in your own games and then we'll have lots of examples which we'll practice together so that you can become a strong chess player.

Right let's get started! We're going to look at some Material Tactics (where you will win material), then some Checkmate Tactics (where you will checkmate your opponent), and then we'll look at some more complex tactics.

Think of tactics as like weapons in your arsenal. The more tactics you know, the more different types of weapons you will have to attack your opponent with or defend yourself with. So let's try to learn as many tactics as possible!

Material Tactics

There are four basic material tactics which will help you win material. They are the fork, the pin, the skewer, and the discovered attack. We will look at these 4 first, and then we will look at more complex material attacks and combinations afterwards.

The Fork

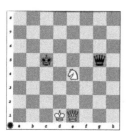

The fork is one of the most basic tactics available. A fork is when one piece attacks two enemy pieces at the same time. In this case the white knight is attacking both the black king and black queen at the same time. We say that the white knight is **forking** black's king and queen. Black's king must move away as it is in check, and white will take black's queen next move, and white will win easily.

The fork doesn't have to be done by a knight either. Take a look at these examples:

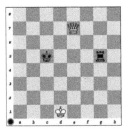

Diagram. White's queen is forking black's king and rook

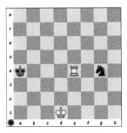

Diagram. White's rook is forking black's king and knight

Diagram. Black's humble pawn is forking white's king and queen!

Ok I think we understand the power of The Fork now. Make sure to use The Fork in your own games. Let's move onto the next Material Tactic, The Pin.

The Pin

The Pin is when a piece attacks an enemy piece which cannot move away. In the above position white's bishop is attacking black's queen, and black's queen cannot move away as it is in front of the black king. White's bishop

58

is said to be **pinning** black's queen, and black's queen is immobile. White will win black's queen for his bishop and white will win easily.

Let's have a look at some more examples of The Pin.

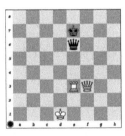

Diagram. White's rook is pinning black's queen

Diagram. White's queen is pinning black's rook, and white will win the rook next move

Diagram. The Pin doesn't have to always be against the king either. In this position, white's bishop is pinning black's rook against black's queen. White will play Bxd5 and win black's rook next move *Pins are extremely useful in chess not only for winning material but also for restricting the movement of enemy pieces by pinning them down. Let's look at the next material tactic, the skewer.*

The Skewer

The skewer is when you attack one piece through another piece. Often this happens when the enemy king is in front of an enemy piece, and by attacking the enemy king you attack the piece behind it too.

Have a look at the following examples:

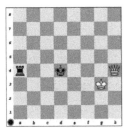

Diagram. In this position, white's bishop is skewering black's king and rook. Black must move his king out of the way and white will take black's rook on g8 next move

Diagram. In this position, white's queen is skewering black's king and rook. Black must move his king out of the way and white will take black's rook on a4 next move

Diagram. In this position, white is skewering black's queen and rook with his bishop on b2. Black must move his queen out of the way and then white will capture black's rook on h8.

Skewers present great opportunities to win material. Next let's look at the 4th and final one of our material tactics, the discovered attack.

61

The Discovered Attack

The discovered attack is when one piece moves away, which unleashes an attack by another piece behind it. Let's have a look at some examples.

Diagram. In this position, white's knight and bishop are in the perfect position to unleash a discovered attack on the black king. It is white's move and he can play Nf3+, where the black king will be in check from the white queen. Black must move his king out of check, and then white can take black's queen with his knight

Diagram. In this position, white's bishop on b2 is on the same diagonal as the black king on h8, and when white's rook on d4 moves out of the way

62

black's king will be in check. White can play Rd8+, attacking black's queen and checking black's king at the same time.

Diagram. Here's an example of both a discovered attack and a pin together. White can play Nd4, getting his knight out of the way of the rook, and unleashing a discovered attack on black's queen which is pinned to black's king. Black can do nothing to prevent himself losing his queen next move.

So those are four basic tactics we can use to win material, the fork, the pin, the skewer, and the discovered attack. Let's do some tactics puzzles now so that we can practice using these tactics.

General strategies

Develop quickly, control the centre (directly or indirectly), don't waste time (eg. move the same piece more than once, don't move your queen out too early, pawn grabbing etc.), get your king to safety, create mini plans to achieve some major goal.

These are some of the strategies to keep in mind

63

For example, if you develop quickly in the opening, control the centre and have a safe king, you'll have more chances or opportunities to make a break in the centre to gain space, to gain space in the flanks, to attack a less developed and coordinated army, to attack a less well defended enemy king and so on. You can choose to do either or all of these strategies where possible.

How you approach the middlegame also depends largely on the opening you choose. For example, if you prefer to play a sharp, tactical game, then opening with the Sicilian Dragon or Open Spanish is a good way to start. If you prefer to a more solid game, then the QGD or the French Defense is your best bet. In general, king pawn openings (1. e4) are more tactical whereas queen pawn openings (1. d4) are more solid and positional.

You can get a rough idea as to who is better in a position by counting the number of points they've captured. Refer to the point chart in *The Basic Rules* chapter. This is actually more important than the amount of material you've captured by your side. As GM Alexei Shirov, once said, "pieces play chess". However, in reality, the player who has the advantage depends on the coordination and effectiveness of their pieces as well as the relative safety of their king.

You may also have heard about how important pawns are in chess. True, Francois Philidor, a very well-known chess player of the 18th century, once said "pawns are the soul of chess." However, is *pawn structure* really that important? It turns out that the answer to this question really depends on what type of position you're playing. Certain traditional weaknesses, like doubled pawns and isolated pawns, can sometimes be useful to have either to bolster defense or to open up lines for attack.

Although pawns are the weakest unit, they are excellent defenders, cost-effective attackers, and can promote to any piece. Their coordination and positioning often influences how well your pieces move and thus how much you can control the board.

Learning some opening traps will help you learn to avoid these, as well as be able to set them up against opponents. Although you shouldn't count on them since most decent players will not fall for them. Reserve these traps when you play blitz or very fast time limits; they often work better under these time conditions.

No one can read minds, unless you are truly psychic, so it's no surprise that you can't really predict what your opponent is going to do. However, you can *anticipate* what they can do and *be prepared* for these options. This is how you should really think when playing chess.

Forcing an opponents' moves in the middlegame is generally not a good idea. Beginners often make that mistake. Whilst many tactics have forceful combinations, the middlegame is not a purely tactical exercise. It is also strategic and positional, and you must learn how to understand these positions and have a 'feel' for them. It's not something that can be taught but after much practice you can achieve it.

Planning an attack

Before launching an attack, you must make sure that your king is safe, **eg.** There are no back rank tricks in the air and that your pieces are well developed enough to attack as well as being able to retreat for defense if necessary.

When you have spotted a weakness in the enemy position, you have a target to attack.

Think to yourself, "Is there a weak square that I can take over? Are there are weak pawns or badly positioned pieces that I can target? Can I directly assault the enemy king?"

If you can say 'yes' to at least 1 of these questions, then you can begin a plan of attack.

In the case of no obvious weaknesses, think about if there are any breakthroughs in the centre, the king side or queen side or any piece sacrifices.

In chess, there is usually more than 1 plan that is acceptable to play so don't be worried about getting a concrete or exact answer. It's better to have a lousy plan than to have no plan at all.

Here are some puzzles to help you learn to plan:

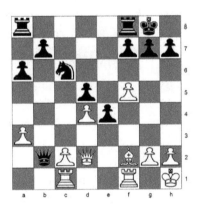

1. White to move

White's queenside has been breached by the black queen and it looks like a-pawn is about to fall as well, unless white decides to defend it with 1. Ra1. However, white's f-pawn is on the doorstep of black's king and the white queen isn't too far away from being able to attack black's king either. What could white play here?

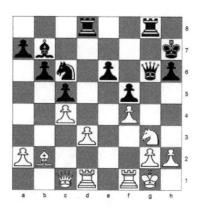

2. Black to move

White's king is looks deceptively safe but once the knight on g3 moves black can deliver checkmate on g2 with his queen. What can black play here?

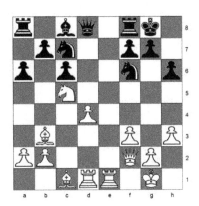

3. White to move

A good example of an isolated queen pawn position (also known as an IQP position). In such positions, the player with the isolated pawn, in this case white, is the attacker and black is the defender. This is because an isolated pawn is a weakness and white must attack in order to compensate for this weakness, otherwise black's slightly better pawn structure will allow him to easily take the advantage. Also having an isolated pawn means more open or semi-open lines that the attacker can play on, so it makes more sense for white to attack rather than to defend.

In any case, the position here looks like White is a little better here. White's pieces are well developed, the knight on c5 looks strong, the bishops are excellently positioned – pointing directly at black's kingside from a distance, the rooks occupy the central files, and the king is safe. On the other hand, black is slightly underdeveloped, the knight on c7 is awkwardly placed and aside from having control of the d5 square, there isn't that much going on for black.

So what can white do here?

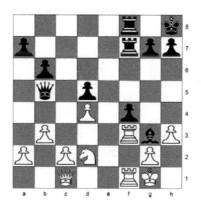

4. White to move

Black has a powerful bishop wedged near white's king on g3 and is causing issues for white to coordinate his pieces. What can white do to get out of this slightly worse position?

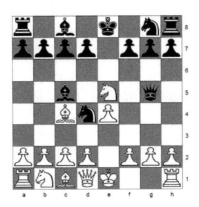

5. White to move

It's only the 6th move of the game but white is already in some danger. The knight on e5 and the g2 pawn are under attack. If white decides to be a bit greedy, it might cost him the game. What are some variations here?

Tactical puzzles

Teichmann, a german master in the early 19th century, once said that "chess is 99% tactics". Clearly an exaggeration, but in some ways, he is right – you need to be able to calculate tactical combinations carefully, no matter what style of player you are. Simply put, tactics are like the bread and butter of chess, is what I would say.

You might go through these puzzles and think, this looks very similar to the planning puzzles since it's just a random chess position and then I have

71

to solve it right? Well, not exactly. With planning, there isn't always a right or wrong answer, just that some answers may be better than others. However, with tactics, there is almost always a concrete answer.

I will give you some examples of what some tactical puzzles look like and their solutions:

Example 1

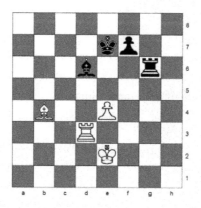

White to move & win

Black's bishop looks to be in serious danger but if the bishops are exchanged (1. Bxd6+, Rxd6), then the game will very likely end in a draw. However, white has a sneaky tricky up his sleeve ...

72

1.Rxd6! (a good move that forces black to take back with the rook, otherwise he'll just be a bishop down for nothing) Rxd6 2.e5! (this move exploits the fact that black has pinned himself by taking back with the rook. Black can play any legal move here and white will simply take the rook with the pawn, leaving white a piece up and a winning endgame) It's a good thing that the bishops weren't exchanged otherwise this trick wouldn't have been possible.

Here's another slightly harder example,

Example 2

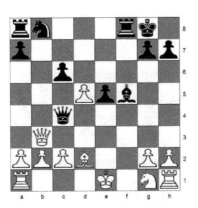

Black to move & win

Although a pawn up, white has pretty much lost the control of the centre and is also behind in development with the king still stuck in the centre. To make matters worse, it also black to move. Black could just take the pawn on d5 with his c-pawn and gain complete control of the centre with 2 connected passed pawns, but there is even a better move. In fact, it leads to checkmate in 3!

1... Qf1+!! (black sacrifices his queen in a forced combination) 2. Kxf1, Bd3++! (a discovered and double check by the rook on f8 and the bishop on d3 – a very lethal move indeed) 3. Ke1, Rf1# (and the white king has nowhere to run)

So here are some tactical problems to flex that chess brain of yours:

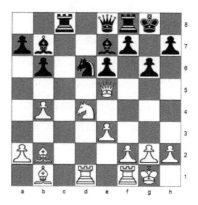

1. White to move & win

White's queen is strong in the centre and the dark squares around black's king are weak. It's only a matter of time before white crashes through.

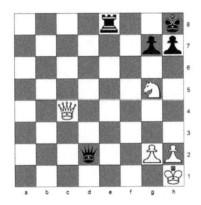

2. White to move and win

On first glance, it looks like black is winning since he is up an exchange, attacking white's knight and is about to mate white on the back rank (aka back rank mate) with 1...Re1+. However, it is white who strikes first and turns the tables around!

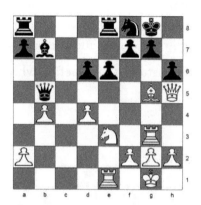

3. White to move and win

White looks like he's in trouble. His bishop is under attack and if it moves, then white's undefended queen will be ready to be taken by black's queen. So this puts white in a real dilemma ... or does it?

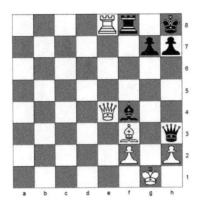

4. Black to move and win

Black looks like he is about to get mated on the back rank. On the other hand, white's king is fairly exposed and if black can somehow find a way to exploit this, he might just save, and even win the game.

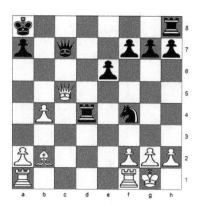

5. Black to move and win

Black's rook is under attack twice and white could win the pawn on g7 if the black rook on d4 decided to move out of the way. However, it is white who should be aware of the danger ahead and not black.

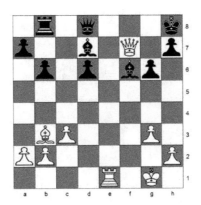

6. White to move and win

White is down a full piece but his queen is dangerously close to black's king. If there was a need for white to do something in order to not lose the game, it should be now.

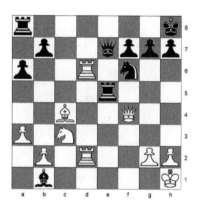

7. Black to move and win

A complex position with many things happening. Black is up 1 pawn, but whites' pieces seem more coordinated. The only major concern for white would be his back rank as it looks a little vulnerable at the moment. Is there a way for black to exploit this?

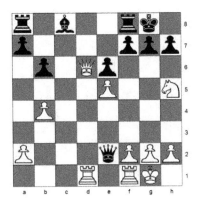

8. White to move and win

Right now, white controls more of the board than black does, although his knight on h5 is under attack. It seems that black's king is fairly safe and there are no back rank tricks just yet. But white does have a winning plan …

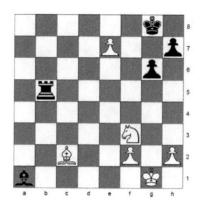

9. Black to move and draw

White's passed pawn is 1 step away from promotion and there is little that black and do to stop it, even though he is an exchange up. Black also must be careful of some traps lingering in the air because of this passed pawn. So what to do for black?

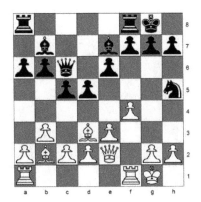

10. White to move and win

Whites' bishops actively placed and pointed directly at black's king. What can white do to shatter black's kingside and have a winning position?

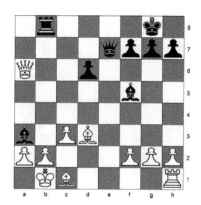

11. Black to move and win

White is under serious pressure here and the white kings' defense is on the verge of collapsing. Can black just put little more pressure on white's house of cards?

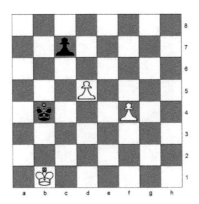

12. White to move and win

Does white's extra pawn count for something or can black hold them both off?

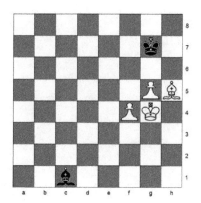

13. Black to move and draw

It seems like there's nothing that black can do to stop both of white's connected passed pawns. Or is there?

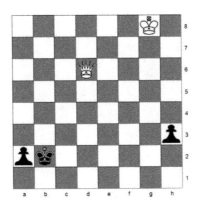

14. White to move and win

White appears to have an overwhelming advantage. 2 pawns stand no chance against a queen (usually). But 2 pawns that are close to promotion might be somewhat of a challenge. Can white actually win this endgame?

Now for the final tactical puzzle, let's finish this off with a bang shall we?

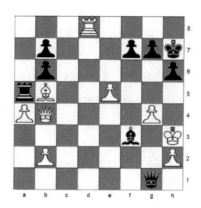

15. White to move and win

White's king looks really exposed and is in fact about to be mated 2 by black. Black's king, on the other hand looks fairly safe and his position is OK overall, aside from the oddly placed rook. What can White do here?

Middlegame Checkmating Patterns

In his book titled *The Middle Game In Chess*, American chess grandmaster Reuben Fine lists three major factors in the middlegame: king safety, force (material) and mobility. If king safety is a serious issue, a well-planned attack on the king can render other elements, like material advantages and tempo, irrelevant. Regarding material, Fine notes that if all other things are equal, any material advantage will usually be decisive. Fine states that a material advantage will usually not give a direct mating attack unless the advantage is very large (a rook advantage or greater).

Strategies for middlegame play often vary. Some middlegame positions have closed centers where both players will need to maneuver behind the lines, while other middlegame positions can be completely wide open, where both players more boldly attempt to gain the initiative. The main principle behind the middlegame in chess is raw calculation. Tactics are a means to an end, and at the bottom they are the means to all ends in chess, but beginner players can't just see tactics as the ends themselves, and this is where positional knowledge comes in handy. Sometimes checkmate can be achieved during the middlegame, but it will require the player to thoroughly analyze the board and look for the key checkmating pattern.

Here are some examples of checkmating patterns in the middlegame.

Smothered Mate – If a king is too well defended for its own good, then he may fall victim to the Smothered Mate. If a king is completely isolated by his own pieces and is attacked by a knight which can jump over the defenders to threaten the king, then the player is in jeopardy of losing the king. A Smothered Mate usually requires a sacrifice and a series of checks to force the opponent to trap his own king.

Anastasia's Mate – Originally seen in the famous novel *Anastasia and the Game of Chess*, Anastasia's Mate is a checkmate involving a rook and a knight along one of the rook files (a or h). This checkmate pattern contains numerous wonderful combinations that can lead to the finale. In this simple diagram, white has just delivered a check with the knight, forcing black to play Kh7 to escape this initial danger. Ultimately, white can checkmate black by playing Rh3#. The rook is stationed on the h-file while the knight blocks the king's path to escape to g6 or g8.

Back Rank Mate – Also known as Corridor Mate, Back Rank Mate is a checkmate pattern that occurs when a queen or a rook checks the opposing king confined in a corridor. When the corridor is located on the back rank, it's typically called a Back Rank Mate.

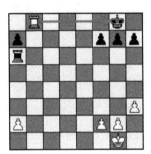 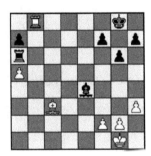

This is considered to be the most common checkmate, and it's also the easiest one to realize, especially after a player castles. Queens or bishops can obstruct the king's passages that are created by the pawns that are directly protecting the king. There is also the possibility of a Back Rank Mate occurring on a column instead of a file. If a player has "doubled up" pawns on the board, his opponent's rook can exploit this opening to checkmate the king.

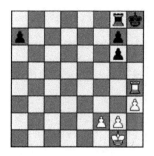 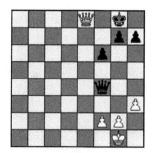

Mayet's Mate – Named after German chess master Carl Mayet, Mayet's Mate occurs when a Rook checks a king adjacent to a corner square under the protection from a queen or a bishop. Looking at the diagram, this is made possible due to the white rook on h1 being on a completely open file and can penetrate the enemy back rank. The dark square bishop on b2 protects the rook on h8 and prevents the black king from moving to g7. The f7 pawn occupies black's only other escape square. Black's pushed up g-pawn exposes the king to dark square bishop attacks.

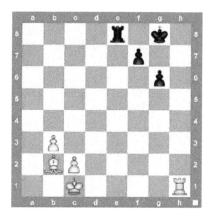

Chapter 5: Endgame

In essence, the complex endgames are those where the general rules are so general that they are useless if the chess tactical ability is deficient. Practically, in the case of complex endgames, general rules cannot be given, and the player's tactical ability continues to prevail.

Most Famous Types of Endgame

King and Pawn against King

This ending can be won or covenant depending on the mutual position of the two kings and the pawn. It is one of the most important endings, either because one of the two players can choose to simplify the game from another position to reach a final that is won (or pact, if the player is at a disadvantage), or because the elements involved in their analysis are often useful for solving endings in which there are more pawns.

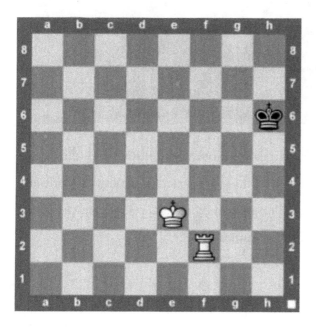

If the opposing king is far enough from the pawn, he can succeed in promoting without the help of his king. The definition of far enough is given by the so-called rule of the square: if the opposing king is outside the square whose side is made up of the boxes in front of the pawn, then it is far enough.

If instead, the king is in the square of the pawn, this needs to be promoted with the help of his king. To quickly establish whether the ending is equal or not, it is possible to use the rule of effective squares. If the king who controls the pawn manages to arrive in the said squares of absolute effectiveness then he will succeed in promoting the pawn, while if he is in those of relative effectiveness the possibility of winning is subordinated to the possession of the opposition (if two kings are found facing each other at a distance from a square, then it is said that the color that must not move has opposition).

If the pawn is a rook (i.e., he is in one of the two sidelines) and the opponent king can place himself on his line, then the match is even, in whatever position the other king is.

Endgames with many pawns

In the endgames of pawns, the dominant theme is the possibility for a king to penetrate in the opposing rows, to eliminate the pawns' adversaries, and thus bring their own to promotion. A crucial element is the zugzwang, that is, the obligation for a color to move worsening its position. For example, leaving a pawn's protection or allowing the opponent's king to gain a cross (for example through the phenomenon of opposition).

In some cases, the kings are both far from the opponent's pawn; in this case, there is a real "promotion race," the result of which is often the appearance of two women on the chessboard. If one of the two colors have at least twice the advantage over the opponent, it has won the match, as it transposes into a queen's final against a won pawn. (See next section).

Queen's endgame

Women's endgames are a very complex type of endings as many plans, although long-term, must be made with precision. Two particular types of particularly important endings are the endgames of kings and queen against kings and pawns, and the endings of queens and pawns against queen.

In the first case, the queen's conductor has almost always won the game, as it can checkmate and simultaneously attack the pawn, forcing the king to make forced moves. If the pawn is advanced to the seventh cross - as it may happen if there has been a "race to the promotion" and one of the two players has some disadvantage - the queen wins if she can occupy the pawn promotion square, or if the pawn is in a central line (d and e) or knight (beg). The strategy consists of obliging the opposing king to occupy the square of promotion, thus gaining a time to approach his king. If instead, the pawn is in one of the lines a, c, f, or h, the game is drawn because of the stall.

Queens' endgames and pawn endgames against queens are very difficult to play and are often very long. The defender must try to reach the square of promotion with his own king, but even if he could not manage, he could still manage. This is true for rook pawns, while for others the queen can check and try to nail the pawn, preventing him from moving forward.

Rooks' endgame

Rooks' endgames are frequent, as these pieces are generally the last to be put into play and therefore those that tend to stay longer. In this case, the central element is the activity of the rook, understood as the possibility of attacking the king and the opposing pawns at the same time or cutting off the king from the area of the board where he can attack pawns.

A particularly important case is the rook and pawn against rook, where the position can be both equal and won by the color that the pawn has, depending on the position. The struggle is centered around the possibility of promoting the pawn, gaining a decisive advantage.

In general, the player at a disadvantage must try to reach the pawn promotion square; the pawn driver must then try to cut it out with the rook or try to reach Lucena's position. Various techniques are possible to apply here, including reaching Philidor's position.

97

If the pawn is in a rook line, the draw opportunities increase significantly.

Bishops' endgames

In the endgames in which, in addition to the pawns, only bishops are present, the color of the bishops (i.e., the color of the squares on which they move) is of vital importance for the evaluation of the position. While in fact, in the case of same-colored bishops the position is more favorable to the attacker (i.e., the player with more pawns or with the initiative), the endgames with bishops of opposite color are infamous for being very often pacts.

The opposite-colored bishops allow reaching the draw also with two pawns of disadvantage, although the presence of other pawns can favor the attacker which can threaten them. On the other hand, only one pawn, is never enough to win (even with same-colored bishops) as it is possible for the defender to sacrifice his bishop on the pawn, thus simplifying a final pact.

In some situations, the bishop cannot win even with the help of a pawn, and with the opponent reduced to the king only. In case the pawn is a rook, and his square of promotion is the opposite color to that of the bishop, and the adversary king can reach it, there is no way to force him to abandon it. The approach of the king causes the stall.

Knights' endgames

These are characterized by the maneuvers of the knights to catch pawns. In the case of past pawns, the knights generally have difficulty trying to capture them, while they are more effective in blocking them. An important factor is also the impossibility for the knights to lose time because moving cannot maintain control over the squares that are attacked.

The final of kings and two knights against kings is always covenant, precisely because the knight cannot waste time. Instead in the final of kings and two knights against kings and pawns the part that has the two knights can win in certain positions. This ending was analyzed in detail by the Russian student Aleksej Troickij.

Queen against other pieces

The queen wins against a rook alone. Even two pawns (if not connected) may be insufficient to fit the game unless one can reach a fortress with one of them. With three pawns you get at least one draw, and in some situations, the rook wins. Two rooks are generally worth a queen. Without pawns, the position is generally a draw, although in some positions it can be won by one of the two players. Generally, two pawns are required to win.

The queen easily wins against a single minor piece, while with two pieces – a rook and another minor piece skated against a queen – a fortress can be built. If the queen's driver has a pawn she can win, while rook, minor piece, and two pawns can bend the queen's resistance.

Rook and minor pieces

In the case of a rook against minor pieces without pawns, the position is generally drawn. A pawn advantage gives the rook advantage, which sometimes is insufficient to win. The rook can win in some situations even with a disadvantaged pawn, but with two it can lose. More pawns often guarantee victory to the minor piece.

In the case of rook and a light piece against rook (without pawns), the match is a theoretical draw (except some positions). However, if the piece is a bishop, the defense is difficult in real play and practice. If the attacker succeeds in entering the position of Philidor he has won the match, although it cannot be reached forcibly.

Chapter 6: Finals: How to handle it

The most helpful tip available in this book to keep improving is this: find more opponents and keep playing chess! Playing with new people will get you familiar with many different openings, styles, and strategies. Some players favor attacks, sacrifices, and precisely challenging positions. Some others play an almost Zen-inspired style of chess, moving around you like water. They can defend against your every attack and they can find a way to compromise your position as a way to improve their own.

There is a term that high-level players use to describe their ability to play chess well and that is their *'chess awareness.'* The more games of chess you play, the more you give your brain a chance to develop pattern recognition, and a chance to improve next time.

It is vital to you, as an aspiring player, to get a chance to play against opponents with different skill ratings as well. Playing with opponents who are better than you gives you a chance to challenge your understanding of the game as well as learn some new tricks or traps that you've never heard before. Another great aspect of playing with different people is getting to meet new friends with a love for the game. Talk about your favorite styles and tactics, and you will find that your overall game sense will improve dramatically.

101

Join the chess community through any of these ways listed below:

Join a Chess Club No, seriously, join a chess club in your area! This is a great way to meet new players and probably new friends too. Most major cities boast at least one major chess club and cater to players of all skill ranges. They host events for children, as well as tournaments for those who wish to test their competitive mettle. The local chess club is a fantastic resource to learn more about the game as well as meeting potential coaches and mentors that are willing to help you grow as a player.

Find a Mentor or Coach Along with joining a chess club, you can try and find a mentor. Someone from a local chess club or tournament with some experience that is willing to take you under their wing and show you cool tricks and tips about the game. These people can offer you a literal lifetime of knowledge to draw upon and are *invaluable* to you as a growing player.

Play in a Local Tournament Along with joining a chess club, this is another great way to enter into the exciting world of chess. At a local tournament, you will meet players of *all* skill levels, and it is another fantastic way to make friends and learn more about the game. After playing a match for real in a tournament, you will find others you can talk to about your matches to help teach you ways you could have played the game differently and a whole variety of ideas so you'll do better next time. Also, because you are playing several games back to back with time in between, it's a great way to try something else different, learn new skills after your game, and apply those new skills in the next round.

Some of the biggest names in chess history started in a small local tournament with a passionate love for the game before they became world-renowned talents.

Chess Puzzles It's been mentioned a couple of times already in this book, but it really must be stressed how amazing these little puzzles are at teaching your brain to think about chess from a different perspective. Going back to the principle of *chess* awareness, these compositions are designed precisely with this in mind. They will teach your brain a fundamental lesson about the way the game works, even if it's only on a subconscious level.

Play a few chess puzzles every day as part of your routine. You can find them on chess apps for your phone, or from the dozens of chess websites out there. The point is to get your brain thinking critically about positions and determining what is the best possible move to make.

Study the Opening If you haven't done so yet – definitely you should study the opening moves of chess. Check out our other book in this series, 'ChessOpenings for Beginners.' In this book, we will discuss the most common openings you will see in a game of chess. The general principles about opening moves to help guide you, as well as extensive theory and research behind the most common moves to open the game.

Understanding when you should make these moves and why, will help you become a better chess player, and help you to enter the mid-game from a solid position.

EndGame Study The last part that will drastically help you close out more games and draw victory from a losing position is developing your endgame knowledge. This is much like studying the opening, in that it is mostly about the memorization of positions, rules, and principles to the end game. Because so many of the pieces are removed, this is a part of chess that can be definitively calculated to an exact degree. Sometimes players view an endgame differently and will proceed to it with a decision based on information which could potentially be flawed. The player that can correctly interpret the outcome of an endgame at a given point is more comfortable deciding whether or not to accept a trade and simply the take position down to an endgame.

This is another one of those elements of chess for which countless books have already been created to help analyze the endgame extensively. This is quite boring, but it can provide very tangible results to help you close out more games. There are many chess puzzles that focus on the endgame if you find that more manageable but do take a look at the endgame in some way or another.

104

How to master the secrets of the masters

Chess is said to be an art and not just a game. Whether you are an expert, a strategy teacher, a technical teacher, or just a beginner, there is always something new and creative you can try. The secret is to be able to detect your opponent's movements in excellent, sharp, and fast planning. This is the beauty of chess. It never gets boring because there is always this challenge. The diversity of movements in the game is almost endless, which is not the case in most table games.

In chess, there is no luck, good luck or luck. Chess refers to skill, concentration, maneuverability, and what we call intuition. The ability to think and plan for your competitors is essential.

The old Greek phrase, *"you know yourself,"* applies a lot to chess. Perhaps I should state the game, yet the player. Know yourself; A great comprehension of your identity is essential for turning out to be what you need to be. Right now, to turn into a top player. However, being the best player does not just mean making decisions, but knowing how to make decisions, why you make them, and how brave you are! You need more than luck to succeed in the affiliate business. Don't rely on the game and nothing else. If you are closed, you will lose it! Of course, some like to play defensively, and that's fine.

When moving, the focus should be on the foot position. Most of the field games are played here, and you have to play defensively at least for a while. Be vigilant and look for openings that you can cross. Try not to change parts as much as possible. Block and wait. Sooner or later, you will have a chance to continue the attack! If you can live with the idea of a chance to win, then let your game become aggressive, strengthening your tracks. If you play this kind of strategy, you have to put your hope in the knights.

Here you can see how your knights can create an open space for bishops and their queens. Fun can be used by infantry to attack. This strategy is often used successfully by many chess "guru," and you will follow this wisely. That said, you should try to play the game only in the way your character does. Not all of us are the same—some people like sweet, others like bitter. If you are a risky person, such as living on the edge and enjoying the thrill of the adventure, then be yourself!

Make a battle opening move and try to destroy the center of the board. Don't worry about replacing the parts but be careful to keep the rook and queen later.

This particular method by which someone aggressively changes parts is called the "butcher's method." This opponent forces you to leave your king and then attacks by attacking where the king is.

My recommendation is to rehearse the nuts and bolts of chess in the most ideal manner conceivable and play your game however much as could be expected, playing increasingly experienced rivals. The familiar adage "iron hones iron" is never more exact than chess.

Study the popular techniques played by the extraordinary chess bosses and consider their reasoning procedures. At that point, go out and do likewise on the off chance that you can!

It wasn't worth less than your full potential. Don't forget to develop your style, movement, methods, and strategies. Take this into account. If you know yourself - and believe in yourself - you will have a perspective on your opponent. This is the key to winning the chess game.

Chapter 7: Tactics to Support Your Strategy

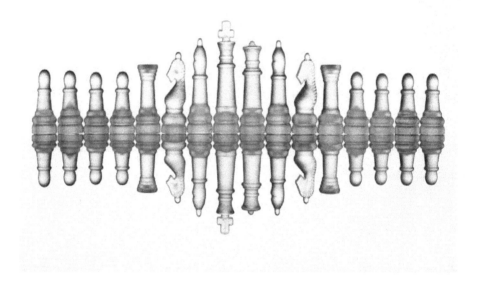

Chess is more about methods. Therefore, you have to improve your chess method. "Chess is ninety-nine percent strategic," stated Richard Teichmann, a celebrated German chess instructor, in 1908, and he couldn't be more correct.

Tactics play a major role in all chess video games and are the vital factors of any method. An approach is a general sport plan; sentences approximately in which you need to be at any factor throughout the match.

108

The tactic is used to enforce a method. Your opponent will no longer sit down and watch you lead your approach without objections. The tactic is used to force your opponent just to accept your actions. The tactic suggests one or more movements to benefit a short-time period advantage. These are fundamental steps in advancing a well-known strategy.

Many processes can be memorized or learned and applied if necessary. By setting greater techniques, the player's arsenal becomes stronger. Learning new processes, if you have to work on tactics and what aggregate of tactics works satisfactorily collectively, is a non-stop activity for the duration of a player's life.

Here are a few common processes that are worth practicing.

Battery Attack

When you think of Battery Attack, imagine a regular electric battery ... each battery is powered by electric cells. If you want more control, you have to acquire extra cells. In chess, a battery attack is formed on the rows (ranks and files) by gathering rooks and queen, while, diagonally, a bishop and a queen are stacked. Unless this is done, the opponent wields more power.

Both the players can use different pieces in their battery attacks.

However, assume the White battery includes 2 Rooks, at the same time as the Black battery includes 2 Rooks and a Queen. Black has a stronger battery, and White is smart to consolidate his 2 Rooks and thus, prevent an assault.

Block

The block is a shielding tactic and is used whenever a bishop, a rook, or an opposing queen manages to govern their king.

In such circumstances, you may try to wiggle through with the help of your pawns or other pieces, to the center of the opponent's attacking unit and the king- take a look at the block and shield the king at least temporarily.

Be aware, and even if your block unit includes the king or other infantry or support devices, the attacker may determine to marvel the blocker in a sacrificial maneuver that has been recorded to remove some of your king's defense.

Authorization

It is also called "easy cleaning", which better describes what's happening here.

Imagine you need to establish your hold on a selected square to reinforce the assault you ride. The problem here is that one your pieces is already in that square.

The issue right here is that transferring that piece ends in its recording. However, due to the superior function, you may get via getting the other piece in that square, it's miles really worth "clearing" that block of the piece, accepting its sacrifice, to compensate for the harm you need. If the answer to this is positive, you may decide to go ahead with the move.

Angry

Decoy includes sending a rifle or sniper rifle to a particular area as a sacrifice to capture the enemy.

After that, your "real" aim is reached, as the "wait" piece gives you the threat to seize the enemy king or exploit every other major part of your rival (normally the queen).

Deviation

Imagine throwing a stone with sufficient pressure at the back of it on every other rook.

When it strikes, a stone with much less strength "deviates" from its resting function. In chess, you can create an attack, and there is enough weight at the back of it (as helping pieces) to assault the enemy's function as a sure factor, and this forces your real target, simply because the king's enemy, to escape from your current attack. The "lost" king moves away from the attacked square and places you in a stronger role.

111

The famous continuous Checkmate is called "Leg all's Mate," which includes Deflection.

Discovery of the Attack

This tactic requires the cooperation of 2 pieces. One can be in the front of the other; one at the backs of the hidden unit is ready to be observed or "discovered." At the chosen moment, the piece moves forward - essentially to release an attack to another pawn/enemy piece, and the last tune is revealed, attacking every other pawn or enemy part (this is not the king's enemy) (more on this in the next tactic.)

Following the attack, the opponent would have to choose to shop or attack the pedestrian to shop. Another attack will attack you. On a defensive note, earlier than making the following move, read the painting and observe your opposition's pieces if you see portions within the neighboring squares (as nicely as each is sitting diagonally, aspect by way of aspect), the first appearance back separately and comply with the down line of the military on the path of your navy. If you hit one in all your portions and if the enemy's enemy is within a variety of your other forces, your opponent may try to smash you with a complete-blown assault.

Discovery Revealed

It consists of principles similar to the attack detection standard. The main assessment is that the adversary of the ruler is one of the portions assaulted.

Since the king is assaulted, his position will be compromised. This implies the king has to be protected no matter what.

The checks were meant to capture the "other" adversary casualty.

Fork Attack

At the factor, while a pawn or piece assaults (at least two) for devices with a solitary move, it is known as a "fork attack".

Fork assaults may be "relative" or "outright".

The relative forks assault as a minimum of two foe units, but no longer the adversary ruler.

Outright forks attack at the least adversary units, and this time, one of the foes pieces is the ruler. At this point, while this is a relative assault, the participant can pick which piece to spare and which to depart helpless earlier than the aggressor.

At the point when this is an outright attack, the participant's top piece ought to be protected, as in taking a look at. The pawn/pieces/exclusive pieces are assaulted by way of their destiny.

113

Conclusion

Thank you for reading this book. For those who are ready to take time to learn the art of chess, they will soon discover that improvement comes easily at the beginning. Mastering some basic techniques and tactics makes a difference between a beginner and a professional player. No individual mental facilities are required to play a great chess game and have an excellent time doing so.

That being said, playing well with chess involves the exercise of your brain. Chess involves attack and defense, tactics and strategy, ability, experience, and patience. You try to implement your scheme while discerning and suppressing your opponent's strategy. You know your adversary is doing the same thing, and you're trying to fool him. The dodge on the wing portrays the actual approach of a middle thrust or vice versa. For these purposes, it is claimed that General Douglas Macarthur advocated the development of chess as a required subject for military officers in training.

Chess is a test of endurance, courage, determination, and concentration. This improves the ability to communicate with others. It tests your athletic skills in a competitive environment.

Chess complements schoolwork and education. Numerous studies have shown that children have a higher reading level, a higher math level, and a higher overall learning ability as a result of playing chess. For each of the

114

reasons listed above and more, chess-playing children do better at school and thus have a better chance of success in life.

Chess is opening up the world for you. You don't need to be a top-ranking player to reach big competitions. Even tournaments like the US Open and the Australian Open accept players of all abilities. Chess offers you plenty of opportunities to travel not only around the country but also around the world. Chess has a universal language so that you can communicate with everyone around the world on an even ground.

Chess helps you to meet a lot of interesting people. You're going to make life-long friendships with people you meet through chess.

Those who are ready to delve deep into the mysteries of chess are rewarded with a perpetually stimulating and fulfilling hobby.

Chess isn't a sport like several others, and its battles are classic. There is continually a subordinate and a war of excellent and evil. It is a game with a first-rate approach and problematic traps and attacks. The chess set focuses on the concept that the king is the most treasured chess piece on the chessboard. If each player declares the check, the priority is to defend the king at any cost. If you can't save the manipulate king, the game is over, and you lose a verification officer.

As a whole lot as chess is a method of recreation, your attitude is excellent. He is almost continually a player who performs a chess recreation if his mentality is dangerous. There is a connection between seriousness and focus, so the more serious you are, the better targeted you're.

Another awesome manner to enhance your chess is to play quite a few games. The more you play chess and the extra experience, the greater you may learn and grow to be familiar with the sport. The extra you play, the more you will begin to investigate your moves and techniques at a whole new level, as your brain reminiscence has improved.

Utilizing chess machine guidelines can help you in improving your sport and provide your adversary with a favored position. Note that everything works; practice every open door you have, and you'll see a huge improvement in your recreation.

Good luck.